Who Are They?

To Sandi,
For everything—KM

To Paul,
For all those burritos, tacos & yummy chili–SM

Text © 1999 by Kris McDonough
Illustrations © 1999 by Sylvia Myrvold

For information address:
McMyr Publishing,
777 First Street #142,
Gilroy, California 95020

FIRST EDITION

Library of Congress Catalog Card Number: 99-90269

ISBN — 1-893849-00-7 (paperback)
ISBN — 1-893849-01-5 (hardcover)

Mc Myr
Publishing

Who Are They?

Kris McDonough *Illustrated by* **Sylvia Myrvold**

O ne morning as I was getting ready for school, Mom said, "Bring your umbrella. They say it's going to rain."

"Who?" I asked.

"*They*," Mom smiled.

"Now get going or you'll miss your bus."

On the way to the bus I wondered, who are *they*?

Are they a bunch of weathermen

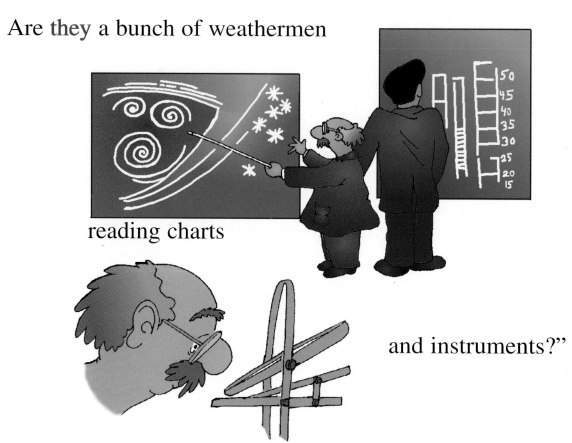

reading charts

and instruments?"

2

On the bus my friend Josie pointed to
an old boarded-up house.
"*They* are going to tear down that house," she said.
"Who?" I asked. "The weathermen?"
Josie gave me a strange look and started talking to Sarah.
I decided maybe *they* were some construction workers
that my mom heard talking about rain.

At school Mrs. Watson said
"Today, class, *they* are giving hearing tests
in the speech room."

"Who?" I asked.
"The construction workers?"

Mrs. Watson gave me a strange look
and the whole class laughed.
Then a gust of wind came
in the window and
blew the door shut with a

and then everybody forgot my question,

so I *still* didn't know who ***they*** were!

5

Our class went together down to the speech room.
Now I could see who *they* were.

In the speech room there were
3 ladies with **3** machines
with big headphones plugged into them.

When it was my turn I sat with the closest lady.
She had a name tag on that said
'Rebecca Meyer, Audiologist'. . .

. . . so I knew she wasn't *they*.

"Who are *they*?" I asked.

She glanced around. "Oh, just the people I work with.
We're testing the whole school today."

I could hardly believe it! Just those two ladies were *they*?
They were as old as my **grandma**!
I had to see if this was right.

"I hear *they* are tearing down that old house on Baker Street,"
I said casually.

"That's right," said Rebecca Meyer,
Audiologist.
"They are building our new
offices there."

Then she put the
big headphones
on my head.

I raised my hand whenever I heard the

beeps and **boops**

in the headphones,
but I couldn't take my eyes off those two ladies.
When the hearing test was over,
I tried one more test of my own.

9

"Hey!" I hollered over to the ladies.
"How's the weather?"

They both looked up, a little surprised,
then smiled at each other.
"Looks like rain," said one,
and the other nodded her head in agreement.

10

My mind was spinning on the way back to class.

Could they really be *They*?

How did they do all that stuff?

How could those
two ladies tell the weather,
give hearing tests, tear down
houses and build office buildings?

I was more confused than ever.

After lunch I found Josie playing dodge ball.

Josie was smart.
She could tell me who they were!

"Hey, Josie!"

I hollered into the circle.
"Let's walk home after school."

"I can't," she said, spinning away from one bouncing ball and jumping over another one. "My mom wants to take me clothes shopping. *They* are having a sale at Diddley's Department Store."

"Who?" I asked.
"The hearing test ladies?"

Josie stopped dead and looked at me
with her forehead all wrinkled up.
A ball bounced off the back of her head.

**"Ha ha,
you're out,"**
laughed Ronald Rinkman,
who threw the ball.

**"Am not!
No hitting
in the head!"**
shouted Josie.

"Out, out! Out, out!"
Ronald chanted and danced
around.

Josie pushed Ronald
and Ronald pushed Josie
and the whole dodgeball game turned into
pushing and shouting
and the bell rang to go back to class...

... and I was back to not knowing who *they* were.

Math class was right after lunch. It started raining and storming and all I could do was stare out the window. I thought and thought, but I wasn't getting anywhere with the *they* problem. It didn't seem to bother anybody else. Did everybody know the answer but me? How did I miss it? Was it a secret? Maybe it was in a packet we took home from school. Was I sick that day? I had a school calendar in my desk. Every morning I put an X through today's date. I checked to see if I had missed any days. Wow! I was surprised to see I had perfect attendance. So we couldn't have had it in school, because I was here everyday. I wouldn't have missed something like that, because I always pay close attention in class and that wouldn't get by me, and besides...

Mrs. Watson said, loud enough to make me jump.

Uh oh. I missed the question.
It was math class, so I guessed,

The whole class laughed.

"Jennifer, math class was over ten minutes ago.
We're on English now."
"Yes, Mrs. Watson."
"Now," she said, "the question is,
does this mean what it says?"
She pointed to the blackboard where she had written,
It's raining cats and dogs.

I looked out the window.
There was a whole lot of water, but no cats or dogs.
"No, Mrs. Watson."

"Now, Jennifer, can you think of other things
that don't mean what *they* say?"

There was **that word** again!
Something inside of me snapped
like a rubber band.

"*They*, Mrs. Watson?

My mom says,
  '*They* say it's going to rain.'

Josie says,
  '*They* are tearing down a house,'
          and
  '*They* are having a sale.'

You say,
  '*They* are giving hearing tests,'
          and
  '*They* don't mean what *they* say.'

Who?
Who are *they*
and how do *they* do all those
things?"

I must have gotten a little excited, because I was standing up
and I was kind of sweaty when I got done.

The class was really quiet and looking at me kind of funny. Mrs. Watson held her chalk up like she was going to write in the air. She was staring at me, and then kind of staring through me.

I got nervous and sat down. I looked at my desk and drew a little doodle. I tried to think of what I would tell the principal when I was sent to the office.

Finally Mrs. Watson spoke.

"Excellent example, Jennifer!" she said. "Most of us use these expressions all the time without really thinking about them. Of course, what you're pointing out in your funny and dramatic way is just a shortcut of speech. It's understood that '*they*' doesn't always mean a specific person or thing. Very good, Jennifer, thank you!

Now, can anyone else give us an example. . ."

Of course!
It's understood!
And **I** pointed it out.

Maybe I'll be a teacher someday!

24

When I got on the bus after school the rain had stopped. The clouds were breaking up and the sun came out.

The old house on Baker Street was flat on the ground in a million pieces, and there were a whole bunch of workers clearing it away to make room for the new office building that was going to be built there.

I saw Josie and her mom going into Diddley's, through the big SALE signs around the door.

My dad met me at the bus stop
with a fresh chocolate chip cookie and a big hug.

"Gee, Dad! Why so nice?" I asked.

"Aren't you my favorite first-grader?"
he asked me back.

"Well," I said, taking a bite,
"that's what *they* say."